First paper-over-boards edition, 2005
1 3 5 7 9 10 8 6 4 2
Originally published under the title *McDuff's New Friend*.
This book is set in Cochin.
Reinforced binding

ISBN 0-7868-3811-6
Library of Congress Cataloging-in-Publication Data on file.

Visit www.hyperionbooksforchildren.com

McDUFF'S
CHRISTMAS

ROSEMARY WELLS • SUSAN JEFFERS

HYPERION BOOKS FOR CHILDREN
NEW YORK

It was Christmas Eve.
Lucy and Fred and McDuff scanned the snowy skies
for a glimpse of Santa Claus's sleigh.

"Santa might not make it through this storm," said Fred.

They put out a thermos of cocoa and shortbread sugar snaps
for Santa when he came down the chimney.
But nothing came down except the howling winter wind.

Lucy walked McDuff in the snowy garden.
Fred gave the baby a bottle.
"The baby is full," said Fred.
"McDuff is empty," said Lucy.

They fell asleep to the snowing and blowing of the snowstorm.

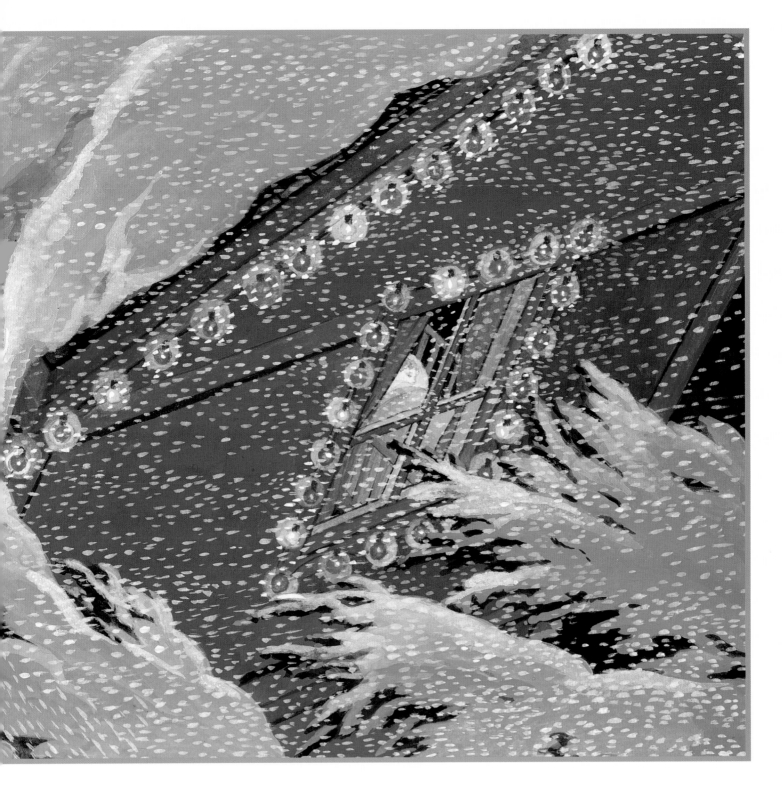

Suddenly something thumped in the night.

McDuff looked out the window with his ears in the radar position.
"Woof," said McDuff.
Lucy woke up. No sleigh bells jingled.

Fred woke up. No one was swooping down the chimney.
McDuff woofed at the door to go out.
"The snow is over your head. You need a dog tunnel," said Fred.

Fred dug McDuff a snow tunnel.
McDuff went to the end of Fred's tunnel,
but the thump was gone.
He came in all wet and snowy.

Lucy fell asleep. Fred fell asleep.
Soon McDuff heard tapping far away in the night.
"Woof!" said McDuff.
"It must be Santa this time," said Fred.

But the stockings were empty,
and no one had eaten the shortbread sugar snaps.
McDuff scratched at the door to go out.
"Not again, McDuff," said Lucy.

Fred had to dig a fresh tunnel.
McDuff went to the end. The tapping was gone.
"McDuff, your sweater is soaking,
and my galoshes have holes in them," said Fred.

"No more woofs in the night, McDuff!"
They all went to bed again.
McDuff was very good and quiet.

Then he heard a squeak and said, "Woof!"
"McDuff," Fred said, "I am not digging any more dog tunnels.
You will have to go out by yourself."

McDuff disappeared in a world of snow.
"Where is he?" asked Lucy. "Oh, I wish I had binoculars!"

Fred put on his wet galoshes with the holes
and followed McDuff's tunnel straight to the garage.

"Holy Toledo!" said Fred.
"I'm stuck!" said Santa. "Where is your snow shovel?"
"I've got it," said Fred. "I've been digging dog tunnels."
"Holy Toledo!" said Santa.

Santa and Fred and McDuff dug the sleigh out of the snowdrift.

Lucy had hot soup and sandwiches
waiting for them when they came in.

"It's almost Christmas morning," said Santa.
"Forgive me if I eat and run."

In Fred's stocking were new galoshes.
In Lucy's stocking was a pair of binoculars.
In the baby's stocking was a pink and blue hippopotamus.

McDuff's present was a new friend.

She drank three eggcups of milk in a row.
Then she settled against McDuff's warm side.
And everyone slept until Christmas afternoon.